Best Wishes,
Cynthia Whipple 2010
&
Mary Cashman

To Ava, Alec, Christopher and Ellena,
our inspirations and our hearts.
To Tony and Doug,
your love and support helped
make this dream come true.
To our parents, love forever.

xo Mary and Cynthia

Merrilee Mannerly™ and Her Magnificent Manners
Text copyright © 2008, 2010 by Mary Cashman & Cynthia Whipple
Illustrations copyright © 2010 by Meredith Johnson

Printed in the U.S.A.

For information, visit www.merrileemannerly.com

Library of Congress Cataloging-in-Publication Data
Cashman, Mary & Whipple, Cynthia
    Merrilee Mannerly ™ and Her Magnificent Manners / written by Mary Cashman & Cynthia Whipple;
    Pictures by Meredith Johnson - 1st ed.
    Cover design, book design and production by Cathe Physioc - 1st ed.
    Merrilee Mannerly™ logo design by Cashman+Katz Integrated Communications

    p. cm.

Summary: Merrilee Mannerly teaches Princess Posy that learning good manners can be both fun and funny.
ISBN 978-0-615-36448-3
[1. Manners and customs - Fiction. 2. Princesses - Fiction. 3. Imagination- Fiction]

[E]-dc22

Printed by BookPrintingRevolution, Minnesota / U.S.A.

Merrilee Mannerly™

and Her Magnificent Manners

WRITTEN BY

Mary Cashman
and
Cynthia Whipple

ILLUSTRATED BY

Meredith Johnson

Pink&Brown Publishing, LLP

Printed in U.S.A.

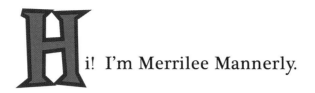 i! I'm Merrilee Mannerly.

You'll never guess who moved in next door...
a princess... A REAL LIVE PRINCESS!

Princess Posy is turning eight, like me.

Today is her birthday,
and she invited me to her party.

A birthday party with a princess!

Here's a secret, though.
This princess is a little different.
This princess has NO manners.

She comes from a land where
NO ONE has manners!

ding dong, ding dong.

"Hi, Nigel," I say to the butler.
"Thank goodness you're here, Merrilee. I think the Princess might
need your help. She's quite different from the last young lady who
lived here," Nigel whispers to me.

Before Nigel can lift his trumpet to announce my arrival,
Princess Posy interrupts him
as she
slides
down
the bannister.

"Merrilee!"

she squeals.
"Come on in.
You're the first
one here."

I look around the room and see an empty table and no decorations.

"Gee, Princess Posy," I say,
"would you like me to help you get ready?"

"Get ready?" she asks.
"What do you mean?"

"Look," I reply. "I brought my grandmother Mannerly's magnificent Manifesto of Manners.

Everything you need to know about manners is in this book.

This will help us get ready for the party.

Now let's see," I say, opening the Manifesto.

Birthday Party Manners

CHAPTER 1

It is good manners to set and decorate a lovely birthday table for your guests.

"Great!" Princess Posy says, digging into a big drawer.
"My decorating kit is right here. I've got... markers
and streamers
and glitter
and ribbons
and stickers and..."

I explain to Princess Posy that setting and decorating a table means
using a pretty tablecloth, plates, silverware and napkins.

Princess Posy and I find what we need,
and we get to work.

Our party table looks **Super!**

ding dong, ding dong.

"That must be my old friends!" Princess Posy says.
"Oh, but you don't know them."

I tell Princess Posy, "Don't worry.
Let's check the Manifesto."

Birthday Party Manners

CHAPTER 2

It is good manners to
introduce a new friend
to your old friends.

Toot!

Nigel announces the arrival of Lady Lulu.

"Excuse me, Nigel," I say. "Princess Posy, you can introduce us by telling us each other's names."

"Girls," Princess Posy says. "this is my new friend, Merrilee Mannerly. Merrilee, I'd like you to meet...

Lady Lulu, Maiden Molly and Duchess Daisy."

"Now that we're all friends,
what should we play?" I ask.

"I know. I have a pony,"
Princess Posy says.

We all run out to the barn.

"Come on everyone. Jump on!"

Princess Posy shouts.

The girls look at one another. They're confused, but since she is their princess, they do what she says and all pile onto the pony at the same time.

"Wait!" I say. "The Manifesto explains this, too."

Birthday Party Manners
CHAPTER 3

It is good manners for each person to take turns when playing party games.

"Sounds easy," the girls say, as they turn and turn and turn and turn and turn and turn and turn and turn and turn

and turn and turn and turn and turn and turn and turn and turn.

"Oh, Princess," I giggle. "Since it's your birthday, why don't you ride the pony first. Then Lulu can go, then Molly, then Daisy and then me. That's what taking turns means."

"That's good," Princess Posy says. "I was getting REALLY dizzy."

Toot!

Just as I get off the pony,

Nigel announces it's time for birthday cupcakes.

We all run into the house as fast as we can.

Princess Posy takes a BIG bite into one of the cupcakes.

"Wait, Princess Posy!" I say. "Look at the Manifesto."

Birthday Party Manners
CHAPTER 4

It is good manners to serve each guest before the hostess begins eating.

"Oh, okay," Princess Posy says, trying to lift
me onto a large silver platter.

"Hey!

What are you doing?"
I ask.

"I'm getting ready to serve you," Princess Posy replies.

"That's funny, but serving a guest
means making sure your guest has
her cupcake before you start
eating yours," I tell her.

"Oh, I get it," Princess Posy says,
laughing. "That's good, because
I'm really not that strong."

We all sit down to eat our cupcakes
and decide these are the best cupcakes ever!

"Let's open my presents now," Princess Posy says.

"Look at me!"

I can't believe how fast Princess Posy
opens her presents.

"Oooh, no...

I already have this," says Princess Posy.

"Princess Posy," I whisper, "here, look at what the Manifesto says."

Birthday Party Manners
CHAPTER 5

It is good manners to show appreciation for every gift and to thank your guests.

"Even if I already have it?" she whines. I nod.

"Thank you for my magic wand, Lady Lulu.

All the presents are open.
I guess that means the party is over.

Bye, everybody!"

"Not quite yet," I tell her. "Look at what the Manifesto says."

Birthday Party Manners
CHAPTER 6

It is good manners to give party favors to each guest.

"Favors!" Princess Posy exclaims. "I can do favors.

Molly, I'll walk your dog for you.

Lulu, I can help you with your homework.

Daisy, I'll clean your room for you..."

"Oh, no!" I tell Princess Posy. "Favors are like goody bags."

Just then, Nigel comes out with a tray of goody bags.
"I was hoping someone would remember these,"
he says, smiling at me.

Princess Posy passes out the goody bags to each of her friends, and everyone hugs goodbye.

After the girls leave, I give Princess Posy my present.

"Wow, thanks!"

Princess Posy exclaims. "This bracelet is super fancy.
Look, it's just like yours."

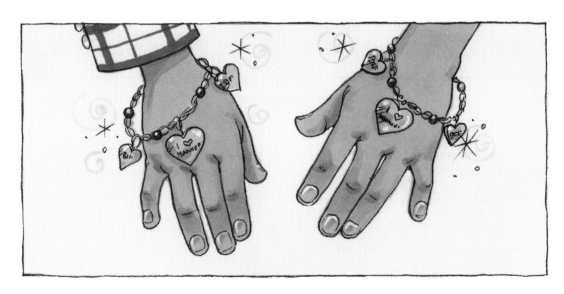

"You're welcome," I say.
"See, good manners are always in fashion."